Anonymous

Maple Hill

Or, aunt Lucy's stories

Anonymous

Maple Hill
Or, aunt Lucy's stories

ISBN/EAN: 9783337328542

Printed in Europe, USA, Canada, Australia, Japan

Cover: Foto ©Andreas Hilbeck / pixelio.de

More available books at **www.hansebooks.com**

MAPLE HILL;

OR

AUNT LUCY'S STORIES.

.

'The lips of the righteous feed many."—Proverbs x. 21.

American Tract Society,

150 NASSAU STREET, NEW YORK.

CONTENTS.

MAPLE HILL.

CHAPTER I.

AUNT LUCY, AND WHY SHE NEVER MARRIED.

"WHAT is an old maid?" asked little seven-years-old Bessie, one day, of her mother.

"What put that question into your mind just now, my love?" asked Mrs. Carrol, with a smile.

"Why, Bridget says Aunt Lucy is an old maid; and that, when she comes, we shall have to walk on tiptoe, and not be able to play at all in the house," replied Bessie.

"How does Bridget know that?" asked the mother.

"She says old maids are always cross, and hate children," said Bessie, with a mournful face.

" Bridget is quite mistaken, my dear. There is not a kinder heart in the world than Aunt Lucy's."

" But what do people be old maids for, mother dear ? " asked the child.

"Because God in his providence makes them so ; just as he makes others wives and mothers."

·" But what do people mean by ' old maids ' ? " asked Bessie.

" It is a rude name for ladies who have spent their youth without being married," replied the mother.

" Well, that's no harm, is it, mother ? "

" Certainly not, Bessie."

" Is my teacher, Miss Morse, an old maid ? "

" Rude and heartless people would call her so," replied Mrs. Carrol.

" And my Sunday-school teacher, too ? "

" Yes."

" Well, then, I don't think it can be such a

dreadful thing, after all, to be an old maid! Neither Miss Morse nor Miss Lake are cross, and I'm very sure they don't hate children," said Bessie.

" They are both noble and lovable women, my child," said her mother; " and as God has laid less care on them than on your mother, they are able to do more good to the little ones who have no mothers. Your Aunt Lucy has spent her youth and lost her beauty in watching beside the sick-bed of my parents. After my sweet mother died, my poor father was ill a long time. He was very aged, and so childish that he was a constant care. But no one ever heard Aunt Lucy complain of weariness or confinement in all those years. When our father died, she mourned for him as deeply as if he had been her strong protector instead of her helpless charge."

" And does she bear with little children, mother, as well as with old people?" asked Bessie.

"She does more than bear with them, my dear. She loves them, and is always doing something to make the poor children around her happy. But you will soon see for yourself what kind of a lady she is. When we invited her to live with us, after the old homestead is sold, it was as much for your sake as for our own. She is such good company, that your father used to say, 'The sun always shines where Lucy is;' so also grandpa, when he missed her from his room, would ask, 'Does it rain?' When told that it did not, he would say, 'I missed the sunshine'!"

"How soon will it be the tenth of the month, mother?" asked the little girl. "I wish it were to-morrow, so that I could see Aunt Lucy."

"You will see her, I hope, in three days, my love. On Thursday morning you and I will arrange her room as nicely as we can, and then ride down to the station for her."

"Mother," asked Bessie, "do you think

Aunt Lucy knows any stories? I have yours all by heart now."

" O Bessie," cried Mrs. Carrol, " I forgot to tell you that she is the very queen of story-tellers! When we were children at home, as you three are now, she, being the oldest, used to relate us the most interesting stories I ever heard. If we were good at home and faithful at school, our reward from this loving sister was a story. Our nursery in the old square homestead had a broad open fireplace. We children, nine in number, used to gather there at nightfall, and form a circle around the blazing logs, — for we wanted no other light, — and listen to her tales. Then we used to sing together, and sometimes tell anecdotes and guess riddles. Thus we spent an hour after tea. Then the three boys younger than Lucy went down stairs to their books, and Lucy would put us to bed, and, holding our little hands in her own, hear our evening prayers. Then she would give us a sweet kiss, and go down-stairs to sew for us long after we were fast asleep. She is still the same sweet unselfish creature, although forty-five years of toil and anxiety have passed away."

"Mother, *you* always put *us* to bed, and hear our prayers, and tell us stories, why didn't your mother do so for her children, instead of Aunt Lucy?"

"Because, my love, she was a very feeble woman, and in those days always had a young babe that required her care at that hour. It was a great blessing to her as well as to us that God gave such a sweet child and sister as Lucy. Do you wonder I love her now, Bessie?" asked Mrs. Carrol.

"No indeed, mother dear; and even if she should be a *little bit* cross, I mean to love her too for being so kind to my dear mother when she was a little girl," said Bessie.

Mrs. Carrol smiled at her affectionate child, and said, "I'm not at all afraid but you'll love her for her own sake, Bessie. She is one of those who carry their welcome in their smile."

"I mean to tell Ned and Jennie all you have said, just as soon as they come home from school," said Bessie. "It will make them happy, I know; for although they both told me she was a very good Auntie, I could see, mother, that they were a little afraid of her, because she was an old maid. You know Neddie took down the swing we had in the garret yesterday."

"Why was that, my love?" asked the mother.

At this moment the children entered.

"Oh, here you are home again, little dears. I was just asking Bessie why you took your swing down, Neddie."

"Because it was right over Aunt Lucy's chamber, and he was afraid it might worry her to hear our feet on the floor," replied Bessie.

"I am delighted to know that my dear boy

was so thoughtful and so polite. It is always proper to regard the comforts of others, especially of guests; and one who does such a delicate act of kindness when only nine years old, will surely make a gentleman when he grows up. I think dear Neddie is trying to fulfill the law of love about which you have been studying. Come here, my boy."

"Will auntie have to be an old maid always, mother?" asked Bessie. "Now that grandma and grandpa are gone, and she is not needed in your home, I should think she might get married; and then she couldn't be called an old maid any more."

"My love," replied Mrs. Carrol, "your aunt has not the least objection to being called thus. She would but laugh at it. It is only silly women, who, having grown old, rebel against what is the lot of all, — who try, by girlish airs and youthful dress, to appear young still, that take offense at mention of this. Still it is very rude and unkind to allude to their situation, because we may wound their feelings without knowing it."

" How, mother ? " asked Jennie.

" Why, my love, we do not know what lies buried in their hearts. Almost every maiden lady I ever knew had some sad reason locked up in her bosom for walking alone through life."

" What is Miss Morse's secret, mother ? " asked Bessie.

" Well, my love, if I could be sure neither of you would ever mention it among the scholars, I would tell you."

" We never will, mother ; for we would not grieve her for anything," said Jennie.

" Well, dears, eleven years ago, — Jennie, it was when you were a tiny baby, — Mary Morse lived in the large house opposite us, and was thought by all her friends to be an heiress. She was about to be married, and had her wedding-dress all ready ; when, to the astonishment of everybody, her father

failed in business. It was through the rash
ness of his partner rather than for any fault
of his own ; but he was so honorable and con-
scientious, that he gave up his own personal
property to his creditors, and began life again
as a clerk in the very store where he had
made his fortune. He was not ashamed to do
so, and probably never dreamed that any body
would be ashamed of him ; but he was mis
taken there. People who esteemed the family expressed their pleasure that Mary was so
soon to have a fine home into which she could
receive the family. But, dear children, although the wedding-day was set, and the wed-
ding-ring bought, poor Mary never saw the
faithless young man she expected to marry,
until a whole year had passed away ! " .

" What had become of him ? " asked Ned.

" He was at home, only ten miles off; but
when he knew there was no money coming to
Mary, he cared no more for her ; and at the
end of the year, when the creditors took pos-

session of the estate, he actually took his bride there to look at it, and bought it at the auction! Now, darlings, do you not think it would be cruel to make any remark to Miss Morse which should bring all this back to her mind?"

" Yes, indeed, mother," said Jennie.

" Why did not Aunt Lucy marry?" asked Ned.

" For the simple reason, my boy, that she *chose* to live single. In her girlhood, she devoted herself to her brothers and sisters, and in maturer years, to her aged parents. Wasn't that noble?"

" Yes, indeed, it was," replied Jennie.

" Miss Morse and your Aunt Lucy are not ashamed of their years," said Mrs. Carrol. " Nobody ever saw them painting their faces to deceive people, but they have learned the rare and beautiful art, how to ' grow old gracefully.' Do you understand that, Jennie and Ned?"

" Certainly, dear mother," replied the eldest little girl; " and I am quite impatient to see dear auntie."

" There is the dinner-bell," cried Ned, springing up and clapping his hands. And with the appetite which fresh air and bright spirits bring, they bounded out to the gate to meet their father, whom they saw from the window.

" Oh, pa, we are so happy about Aunt Lucy's coming to live with us ! " cried Jennie. " Mother has just been telling us all about her."

" Good friends are a great blessing, my dears," said the father; " and your aunt is a lovely woman and a devoted Christian. If you desire to know and love God, you will find her a great help to you. She has had a hard life, but no one would ever learn it from her, —she is always so bright and cheerful. God's will is her will ; so she sees no cause for murmuring."

CHAPTER II.

MAPLE HILL NURSERY.

THURSDAY morning dawned bright and clear, and the little Carrols were up with the larks. While their mother was busied with her morning duties, the children cut baskets full of flowers, with which to decorate the chamber of the dear expected guest. They were allowed the privilege of doing this themselves, according to their own taste; so while the little white fingers of Bessie were busy over the vases, Jennie was festooning the white muslin curtains with roses, and looping them up with garlands of flowers. Childlike, they fancied the more they trimmed the furniture the finer it would appear; so, every conceivable nook and corner was made to hold a vase or goblet, and every glass or picture to

2

bear a wreath. Their mother was surprised
at the neatness and skill with which the work
was accomplished ; and when called up to
give her opinion of it, said, " I really think
you have been partial to your aunt ! How
would you like to transfer a few bouquets
and wreaths to my room, and thus give dear
father a surprise when he goes up-stairs to-
night ? "

The children thought this a charming idea,
and, as it was nearly their school-hour,
gave their mother leave to take out as
many of their decorations as she thought
could be spared from Auntie's room for her
own.

Mrs. Carrol was too wise a woman to crowd
the brains of her young children with every
study taught in schools, caring far more to
have them strong than " forward," as many
wise children are called. Bessie had been at
school one term ; but not being well, her
parents kept her at home now, where she

studied one hour with her mother, and the rest of the day with the birds and flowers. How sweet those lessons were! All nature, whether animate or inanimate, has lessons for man, and these her mother explained to her. When Bessie pointed to an ant-hill, with its thousand little toilers, and stepped aside rather than crush them, her mother would say, " Blessed are the merciful, for they shall obtain . mercy ; " and remind her how the wise man bids the sluggard go to the little ant to learn her ways and be wise. When she came in with delight to say that the lilies had blossomed, she was taught to repeat the sweet words of Jesus to his anxious disciples : " Consider the lilies of the field, how they grow, they toil not, neither do they spin ; and yet I say unto you, that even Solomon, in all his glory, was not arrayed like one of these. Wherefore if God so clothe the grass of the field, which to-day is, and to-morrow is cast into the oven, shall he not much more clothe you ? " Thus, although little Bessie did not go to school, she was gaining every day both health and wisdom.

Well, on this lovely spring morning when all was in order at home, and Ned and Jennie had gone to school, Mrs. Carrol had "Billy Gray" harnessed into the family carriage, and she and Bessie went to meet Aunt Lucy at the railway station.

When the whizzing and rattling of the train were heard in the distance, they both stood upon the platform looking up the road to catch the first sight of its approach. Mrs. Carrol felt very sad, for she realized that the pleasure she expected was only obtained by the death of her beloved parents; and that in Aunt Lucy's leaving the homestead, it was closed for ever as *her home*. Bessie looked a little sad too, for she was not yet quite sure that she should be pleased with her aunt, although well convinced that she was very good. But little hearts ask more than this; they expect

their friends to be also kind and genial in their
manners.

When the cars stopped, Bessie looked among
the passengers for a tall, gaunt, homely lady
in deep mourning; but she looked in vain. In
a moment, however, she saw her mother throw
her arms around the neck of quite a different-
looking person. Mrs. Carrol could not speak,
for the tears which fell fast choked her voice.
But Aunt Lucy spoke in a low, sweet, tone,
smiling through her tears, and asked, " Is this
my little Bessie, whom I named for grandma?" The little girl kissed her, and felt, as
she looked in her fair face, as if she had known
her always.

While they are riding home, we will tell the
young reader how Miss Thorne did look. She
was short and plump, with a face which was
made to smile. Her eyes were of no partic-
ular color, but so clear and deep that you
could see the very heart through them, and
know that all was sincere within. In youth,

she had been handsome, and now, although the clear complexion was marred by time, and the brow lined by a few wrinkles, still the rose bloomed on her cheek; and her fine teeth, which she displayed freely every time she smiled, gave her such a happy, cheerful expression that, but for her bright gray curls, one might almost have believed her yet a girl.

Oh, what delight the Carrol children had in listening to the conversation of their aunt and mother, about the people and the scenes of by-gone days! Before bed-time came, on the first evening after Miss Thorne's arrival, the children had all decided that it was the finest thing in the world to have an aunt to live with them. Ned remarked, that having Auntie there, was "like having company all the time."

"Auntie," said little Bessie, "mother called you the 'queen of story-tellers;' she says the most interesting she ever heard were those you used to tell by the nursery fire when she was little. I suppose you've forgotten them all now, haven't you?"

" Oh, no indeed, darling," cried Aunt Lucy; "my memory is too good for that!"

" How I wish we could hear one of the very stories you used to tell your brothers and sisters!" said Ned.

" O Ned, they would not sound the same to us as they did to ma, in the fire-light, with old Mark Antony the watch-dog and Cleopatra the house-cat snoring and purring on the rug, and so many children gathered round them," replied Jennie.

" Don't your dog and cat snore and purr?" asked Auntie, in a tone so amusing that the children all laughed.

" Oh, yes, but we have no hearth-rug with a meeting-house on it for them to lie on, no wood-fire to light the room, no shining brass andirons to see our faces in, broader than they are long," said Jennie.

"I'm not sure about that," said Aunt Lucy, looking very wise. "We shall see, after I get rested from my journey. Let us thank God, darlings, that he has preserved us all to meet here in your sweet home. I don't know of a greater blessing any one can have in after-life, than the memory of a happy home in childhood. I often sit at my work for hours thinking over the days of my childhood on Maple Hill, and find a sweet relief from present care and trouble. I would not have those scenes and the sweet faces that mingle with them blotted out for all the money old Billy Gray could draw."

"Well, Auntie, when you do get rested enough to tell us stories, will you let me invite Hattie Baxter and her brother Joe in to hear them? They have no mother," said Jennie.

"Indeed I will, my love," replied Aunt Lucy.

"And perhaps," said Mr. Carrol, who had been listening in silence, "you will also admit

mother and me. That would be almost as
large an audience as you used to have at
Maple Hill."

"Oh, I'll let you all in," said Aunt Lucy
in a merry voice. "I think I shall have to
call my room 'the nursery.'"

"But, father, I'm afraid, if you and mother
are there, the stories will be too wise for us;
I'm sure Bessie won't understand them," Jennie said.

"O mother, hear that!" cried Bessie. "I
guess I can understand a good deal; can't I,
mother?"

"Indeed you can, my love. Auntie can
tell stories which will suit us all. I've often
thought that you are interested in the same
books which please Jennie and Ned." .

"Yes," replied Bessie gravely, "and I
never care for stories that begin, 'Once upon
a time.' I like sensible talk as well as other
folks, if I *am* little; don't I, mother?"

"Yes, dear, you do," replied Mrs. Carrol,

while the rest all laughed heartily at the little
girl's earnest defense of her own powers of
comprehension.

"Well, Pet," said Aunt Lucy, "if you don't
understand the first, I will tell one on purpose
for you!"

"But I *can* understand, Auntie," persisted
Bessie.

"So you can, dear," said her mother.
"You know and love many things which wise
men turn away from and of which they die in
ignorance."

Friday and Saturday passed and nothing
more had been said about Aunt Lucy's stories,
and these children were too good to tease and
worry about any pleasure which had been
promised them. They noticed that their aunt
and mother seemed very busy up-stairs on
Saturday afternoon; and that they had some
subject of conversation which they chose to
keep to themselves. So they asked no questions, feeling quite sure that if it were prop-

er for them to do so, they should soon hear
all about it.   How happy such children can
make a whole family !   Obedience and respect win the love of all, and are pleasing
to the Holy One who gives to children their
home and their friends.

CHAPTER III.

RESPECT FOR THE AGED.—THE STORY OF SALLY BROWN.

A COLD summer rain was falling, and the east wind blowing without. After tea and lessons were over on Monday evening, Aunt Lucy said, " I shall be very happy to see any one who wants to hear a story in my chamber now."

Ned caught his cap, and darted off to invite their little motherless neighbors, the Baxters, and Jennie and Bessie waited his return at the front door. When they arrived, they all went up, and, as polite children will always do before entering a private apartment, knocked at the door. Aunt Lucy opened it herself; and with a pleasant smile said, " Walk in, little folks, to the old nursery of Maple Hill!"

The Carrol children looked amazed, hardly knowing where they were. The fire-board — they had forgotten that there was an open fireplace in the house — had been removed, and there, supported on great brass andirons, were sticks of wood burning brightly, sizzling, roaring, and sending up sparks in a way to surprise as well as to cheer modern children on a night like this. On the mantle-piece towered up tall candlesticks, in which candles were burning. Little chairs and stools were placed around the fire, and on these Auntie asked her guests to be seated. What was their amazement to behold the very rug, which they knew by the description used to lie before the fire at Maple Hill ; and on it — looking not a little surprised by this attention — Pompey and Grizzle !

Mrs. Carrol soon explained that the old rug came round an article of furniture which was sent her from her early home; and that she borrowed the andirons and candlesticks.

"Now, then," said the kind aunt, "I am ready to tell you one of my stories. It will be rather hard to interest two such wise folks as Mr. and Mrs. Carrol, and at the same time to please little ones; but I will do the best I can. First I will tell you the story of one I used to know, but whom I never could love after I heard her history. I could give you a more amusing one; but on the whole this seems the best to begin with. It will teach you lessons of respect and gratitude to the aged, a class whom God tenderly regards, and whom he has commanded us to honor. How much my dear mother used to lean on God's promises to the aged! How often she used to say, —

E'en down to old age all my children shall prove
My sovereign, eternal, unchangeable love ;
And when hoary hairs shall their temples adorn,
Like lambs in my bosom they still shall be borne.

SALLY BROWN.

" MANY years ago there stood a humble little cottage in a western forest. A circular spot had been cleared for it, but all around the large oaks stretched out their arms and seemed to grasp each other, thus forming a roof over the lowly dwelling. The blue sky could be seen here and there through the ever-fluttering leaves, and the birds built their nests in the branches and sung merrily there. The leaves of the silver birch kept up their unceasing dance in the light breeze, the wild flowers grew in profusion, and the young pines shed their fragrance around the place. You would have almost thought that little opening in the deep forest to be a scene in fairy land, so laden was it with the beauties which deck that fabled region. But the house which stood within it in no way resembled a fairy palace. Its structure was of the rudest kind, and the shed which stood beside it

looked frail indeed. This sheltered the stock
of the little farm, consisting of a cow, pig,
and an aged horse. The dwelling contained
but one room, and a garret which was reached
by a rude ladder. The room had one window
in front and one behind, and in summer these
were always covered with the meek morning
glory and gaudy nasturtium vine. The little
plot before the door was smooth, and made
soft with the sheddings of the pine for many
a year. Altogether the place wore the aspect
of poverty, but the aged couple who dwelt
there knew it not. They had been poor
through a long life of toil and sorrow; but
now, when their sun was setting, they felt very
rich. By the labor of their own hands they
had built this lowly home for their old age,
and paid for two acres of land surrounding
it. True, the chimney was made of stones
and clay, and looked very rough, and the floor
was of unplaned boards; but, for all this,
many a rich neighbor who smiled scornfully

as he passed might have envied the peace and happiness enjoyed around that unhewn hearth-stone.

" These worthy people had reared a large family, but their children had fallen one by one, till they were left in their old age without one arm on which to lean. But no murmur ever rose from their lips, no doubt ever marred their faith in God's mercy for the future.

" The meek-spirited woman, now too old to toil hard for the neighbors, as she had been wont, plied steadily her knitting-needles, and thus helped to earn the few comforts they needed. Her companion, cheerful and active, although the frosts of seventy winters lay heavy on his head, wove corn baskets for the neighboring farmers. When the light faded away, the old man would seat himself on the broad hearth and plait his baskets by the light of the hemlock branches which blazed and crackled there. Then they talked of their many mercies, and sung songs of praise to

God, who had not left them when gray hairs
were upon them.

"And thus in simple love and quiet faith the
aged pair had lived several years previous to
the death of their last child. She was poor,
and died far from home, where she had gone
to earn her bread. She left a helpless child
with no friend near but a careless and indo-
lent father. He carried it at once to the
grandparents, expecting no doubt a rebuke
for casting it off. But no ; they knew that
he would not rear the child in the fear of
God, and so they were thankful to take her.

"Sally was a sweet and gentle child, and
very soon the old people began to wonder how
they had ever lived alone so long. As she
grew, she learned to lighten in many little
ways the toil of her grandmother, and always
cheered with her singing voice the labor of
the old basket-maker, when he went into the
wood to gather his basket stuff. She loved
to run to the brook near by for a little pail

of water, and to the grove for brushwood, and altogether she was a good and useful child. They taught her themselves to read, for the school was a long way off, so that she could only go a few weeks in summer. But these good people well knew that she ought to learn far more than they could teach her, that she might be useful in the world, and often talked together about it. This surprised Sally, as she had thought her grandparents very wise, and she said, ' Oh, Grandfather, I know a great deal. I can read my primer nearly through, and all the learning I shall need to take care of you will be to read the Bible. If anybody would make a lady of me, I would not go away ; for I should never find such a beautiful home as this, nor any one so dear and good as you and grandma.'

" And thus the bright summers and the cold winters passed away ; and Sally was now fourteen years old. Then came a gayly-dressed cousin from a distant city, to visit the old people. She had been a playmate of Sally's mother, and took much notice of the child. She told her how very handsome she was, and how much better she would look, if she had fine dresses and bonnets. Sally was not a little surprised at this, as she considered her red calico gown with its orange-colored flowers very elegant, and knew how many pairs of stockings she and her grandmother had knit to purchase it. But this new cousin was the greatest lady she had ever seen, so she must be a good judge; and she began to be ashamed of her high-necked and short-waisted dress, which but a week before called forth such simple pride and such gratitude to her grandmother.

" This cousin was the wife of a man who, although coarse and ignorant, had by a sudden speculation grown rich. She had no children of her own, and when she saw Sally, with her sweet face and pleasing manners, she wished to take her home. At first the old people de-

clared they could not part with her, and she,
that she would not leave them to go away with
the queen. But promises were made of giving
Sally a good education, so that in three or four
years she could return and teach the village
school. This seemed to the old people the
highest pinnacle of grandeur, and they gave
a reluctant consent to her departure. The
cousin promised to send Sally regularly to
church and Sabbath-school, and to teach her
the holy lessons of love and truth. But alas
for all these promises! she herself was a
stranger to God's word and to his sanctuary.

" Sally was soon three hundred miles away
from her best friends, and exposed to all kinds
of temptation. At first she used to object to
many things which she feared would displease
her absent guardians. But she was laughed
at, and told that her grandparents were ignorant, backwoods people, who knew nothing
about the gay city. Such remarks at first
deeply pained the young girl, for she felt that

in listening to them she was injuring those who amid great sacrifices had protected her in her helplessness. But the human heart when left to itself is very ungrateful and very deceitful; and Sally, being young, was soon drawn away into vanity, and forgot the words of warning and of prayer she had heard so often at the fireside in the old cot. She soon began to dress like her superiors, and to affect a great many airs which nature never gave her. Then she looked back in scorn upon the happy days she had passed in the depth of that old forest, saying, ' I shall be wretched when I go back to my home again.'

" ' I mean you shall never go back again,' said the rich cousin, ' and I am sorry that the old people seem so impatient to see you. It is of no use to keep writing all the time to them. They will die soon, at any rate; so if you go back, you can not be with them long. Why, there would not be room enough in the whole house for you; — how could you ever climb up that rough ladder to go to bed, after having had such a large chamber all to yourself?' Such were the lessons of neglect and scorn which were daily given to Sally as she grew to womanhood, and they were about all the lessons she received,— gaudy dresses, and gay company absorbing her time and thoughts.

" All this time the heart of Sally was growing harder and harder; but those of the aged friends were beating with anticipation of her return. Week after week they suffered disappointment in not hearing from her, and then they would flatter themselves that she was on her way to them, and thought to give them a joyful surprise. But four long years rolled away, and she had not come. Her last letters were short, and exhibited none of her former impatience to see them. They grew weary and heart-sick from hope deferred. They feared that their own simple letters had failed to express the deep longings of their hearts for her company and care, which they greatly needed. So they opened their hearts to the schoolmaster, asking him to write a letter for them, which he gladly did. Now they were very sure that such an eloquent appeal would bring back an answer speedily. Poor, fond hearts! It was cruel beyond degree thus to cast them off when their strength failed. But Sally, the little outcast child whom they had fondly reared, and over whose sick pillow they had sat many a long night, had hardened her heart to do it. The humble home which had seemed like paradise to them began to look gloomy, and they resolved to sell it and set off in search of their lost darling; for they feared that some evil, perhaps death, had befallen her. It would have been a great undertaking for the young to travel in a mail-coach drawn by four strong horses, several hundred miles; what then was it for this couple, of fourscore years, in an old chaise drawn by a very venerable horse!

" After weeks of travel and weariness, they,

one bright spring afternoon, entered the gay
city ; and we are sure they and their equipage
attracted some attention. They made constant inquiries until they found the street in
which Sally lived. They rode up toward the
house, just as Sally was parting on the steps
with some of her friends. ' Oh, do look at
that old horse and chaise,' she cried ; ' I believe Adam and Eve have risen from the dead ;
or have two mummies from the Egyptian cata-
combs emigrated to this country ?   Do look at
the old man's bell-crowned hat, and at the pile
of capes on his old coat.'   But, as they all
gazed rudely at the modest pair, the old square-
top chaise, with its rude, unpainted shafts,
drew up to the door.   ' Is this Number 13 ? '
shouted the grandfather. Sally turned pale as
she answered him, ' It is.'   He replied with
a smile, ' Then I suppose you are our dear
child, Sally Brown ! God in heaven bless you,
child,—come, help your grandmother out of
the *shay*, for she's a'most wore out.   We was

determined to find you, darling, if alive ; and
if dead, to be buried aside of you.'

" Sally did not move, and the poor old woman
got out as well as she could with her husband's
help, and began to embrace her in the fondest
manner.   Sally's visitors, being mean and
cruel enough to ridicule the aged and poor,
whom the Almighty bids us to honor, had not
of course delicacy enough to leave now, but
stood waiting to have the mystery explained.

" They could scarcely believe it when they
learned that these were the grandparents of
one so elegant as they thought her to be, and
did not fail to spread the news wherever they
called of the arrival of Sally Brown's beggar
friends, and of her mortification at their ap-
pearance.

" The reception which the aged couple me
with at the city cousin's was exceedingly cold
and they soon felt that they must find a home
somewhere else.   Three hundred dollars which
they had procured from the sale of their little

arm enabled them to hire and furnish a cheerful room. But the coolness of their reception
gave a wound to the heart of the grandmother,
which she had not strength to overcome. No
subsequent attention from her niece or from
Sally could erase from her memory that first
cruel meeting. The summer and the long
winter following wore away, and they had
every comfort, but hope had fled from the
cheerful breast of the worthy woman. Her
spirit was crushed, for she felt that the only
being in the world on whom she had a claim
was ashamed of her. Sally *looked* like a lady ;
but if true politeness had had any place in her
heart, she could never have dealt thus with
the aged, even had they been strangers.
Sometimes she called on her grandparents,
and offered to assist them, but said she could
not do much, as she herself was dependent.
But this was her own choice, for God had
given her health and ability to labor ; but she
preferred a life of vanity and idleness to one

of usefulness and gratitude. The feeble pai
felt deeply that she was no longer their child
and her patronizing visits were a restrain
rather than a comfort.

"They were not suffered to be a burden t
any, for before their money was gone they botl
fell asleep. They entered the home wher
the lowliest child meets with a cordial wel
come. 'Come, ye blessed of my Father, in
herit the kingdom prepared for you.' Neve
more can their loving hearts be disturbed b
ingratitude, neglect, or scorn!

"I'm sure, dear children," said Aunt Lucy
" you think that what little treasures these ol
people had, were left to others rather than t
this ungrateful child. But it was not so; the
loved her still, and, cruel as she had been, he
happiness was very dear to them. A hundre
dollars and the simple furniture with whic
they had kept house were left after their fu
neral expenses were paid, and Sally, who no
called herself 'Sarah,' lost no time in turnin

all she could into money.   With this she pur-
chased a watch and chain, ear-rings and gold
bracelets ; so that Peggy Blunt, the old woman who lived in the next room, and who had
done for the old people what Sally should have
done in their sickness and death, said, ' That
are vain cretur has got the cooking-stove
round her neck, and all the rest of the furniture in her ears and on her wrists.'

" How truly does a love of dress and of vain
company blot out sincerity, gratitude, and all
that makes woman loved and blessed.   Beware
of the spirit which tempts the young to indulge
in ridicule and sarcastic jests against those
whom the Lord tenderly loves and watches
over, — against *any* of his creatures.   The
flight of years has made great changes around
the home of Sally's childhood.   The little set-
tlement is now a large city, and the deep forest where the little cot stood is covered with
houses and gardens.   But years can never
change the past for her, nor efface from her

mind her cruel treatment of those faithf:
friends. The memory of those patient b₁
sorrowful faces, we doubt not, often visits h₁
dreams and disturbs her waking hours. Be
ter had it been for her had she spent her li:
with them in simple love and usefulness.

"And that is nearly all I know about Sall
Brown," said Aunt Lucy. "She became a
quainted with a silly young man, who, findir
she despised labor, and had declared she nev₁
would marry a *mechanic*, left his trade -
house-painting — and went into a small dr:
goods store as a clerk. Then they were ma
ried, and Sally, fancying she was a merchant
wife, came out in plumes and flowers and lace
and a great costly velvet shawl! But by an
by these had to be paid for; and then she foun
out that her husband's income was only hal
what it was when he did his honest day's wor
with pot and brush. He soon had to go bac
to them; and then people said he used to sli
out of the basement door, like a thief, with h

paint-pot done up as one package, and his overalls as another. They became very poor, as people too proud to work always must, and then Peggy Blunt said, 'They can eat gold watches and bracelets now!'

"Dear children," said Aunt Lucy, "I have been so long the companion of the aged that I have learned to love them all; and nothing grieves me more than to see one such coldly or rudely treated. Let it be your principle through life to add one grain, if no more, to the happiness of those who are going the down hill of life. You will receive a rich reward in their gratitude as well as in the approbation of Him who has said, 'A hoary head is a crown of glory when found in the way of righteousness.'

"And this is the end of Story Number One! To-morrow night, if we are all spared, I will tell you one not so sad as this; one of a dear child who tried to do all in her power to make others happy. Now a kiss from each, and then away to blessed sleep and happy dreams."

CHAPTER IV.

"What, has evening come so soon again?" asked Aunt Lucy, as her nieces and nephew, the little Maxwells, and Lillie Emerson, another guest, entered "Maple Hill Nursery," as her chamber was now called. "Well, truly time flies; and soon all our days will be gone!"

"Now for the story, dear Auntie," cried Ned, rubbing his hands together impatiently.

"Some people," said Aunt Lucy, "think that little children, and the poor especially, can not do any good in the world. But we will show them what one poor child did from love in her heart."

OLD KARL.

" FAR up among the Swiss Mountains may be seen many little hamlets composed of cottages occupied by humble shepherds and herdsmen. In some of them, the lowly church is surmounted by a cross, as a token that there the Virgin Mary and other saints are worshiped. But it is not so in all, for many of these mountaineers are worshipers of the only true God and Jesus Christ whom he has sent. In one of these secluded villages, down in a deep green valley, stands a little moss-grown stone chapel, with a low square spire. And it is just as well that the spire is low, for the loftiest one could not point up so effectually to God as do those everlasting hills which he has made. As you stand in the humble graveyard, you read the names of the dead painted on boards made in the form of gravestones. There are words of love just as fervent as if graven in costly marble, but

4

they soon decay and fall to the ground. The
people do not earn enough money to enable
them to buy more durable monuments for
their friends, and, as they are satisfied with
these, it is just as well.

" If, standing here, you turn your eyes upward, you see the snows which never melt,
while beneath your feet, the flowers are bloom-
ing and the vine bending under its wealth of
grapes. Summer and winter, seed-time and
harvest, seem to have met and shaken hands
on these beautiful mountains.

" The people in the little hamlet of which
we are now speaking are honest and simple-
hearted, living in the fear of God and loving
each other. There is one house much larger
and finer than the rest, and the man who
dwells there owns most of the flocks and
herds which graze in the valley, and the vineyards with which it abounds. These posses-
sions give employment to most of the cot-
tagers, who, by toil and strict economy, gain

the bare necessaries of life. But in one little stone cot dwells a man whose day of *toil* is over. His long life was passed among these hills. In youth, by teaching the children, and in old age, by loving and amusing them, he had won every heart to himself. When the people at length wanted a wiser teacher than he for their children, they did not rudely cast him off in his old age, but interceded for him with the man at the ' high house,' as it was called, and he became one of his shepherds. Then would the children gather round him before and after school, and listen to his words of kind advice and to his tales of the olden time. The little holiday sports were generally before his cottage door, where he would allow them to deck with wreaths the lambs of his fold, and would himself sit down by the bright spring and share their little feast. Do you think old Karl was simple because he loved children and strove to gather them around him ? Ah, no, he was a very wise man, and did far more good than thousands who teach the wisdom of the world.

"One day a little girl made a wreath of flowers, and, laughing, placed it on the old man's head, saying, 'See, Father Karl, now you are crowned for our king.' He smiled and said, 'My crown is far more beautiful than those which monarchs wear. God alone could make it, but any good goldsmith could make a crown of gold and jewels. Besides, crowns are very heavy, darlings, and not only make the head ache, but also the *heart*, with the weight of cares they bring. Oh, how much I thank God that I am his child, — old Karl, the mountain shepherd, — and not a king or duke.' Then he led their minds away from their play, and talked of Him who wears an immortal crown in heaven, and who might have worn an earthly one, but who, for our sakes, chose to be poor that we might be rich, — lowly, that we might be raised to a seat at God's right hand.

" Karl once had a faithful wife, but she had gone to heaven long ago, so he was quite alone in the world ; but he was not at all anxious for the future, for he said that as his Father owned the whole world, there was no danger that he should suffer or starve. No wonder that the children loved the friend who led them through such pleasant paths to the Redeemer.

" Elise, the little maiden at the ' high house,' loved to listen to his pleasant stories, although she did not know as much about Jesus as did the poorer children, nor love Karl for His sake. She sometimes went to his home in the valley, and gave him warm garments for the winter, and nice food which he could not afford to buy. If she had a little roll or a basket of fruit for him, she would have it carried by a servant, or send for him to climb the steep hill to get it.

" There was another little girl who had the same kind feelings towards the old man, but

she had not the means of showing it in the
same way. Terese's father was poor. ´ He
had a good flock of sheep, the wool of which
helped to clothe the little ones in winter.
Every week he killed a lamb, but as he had
no horse to carry it to market, Terese and
her brother took it in baskets four miles. In
summer they went through the road to the
nearest town, and in winter they strapped
their baskets to their shoulders and skated
there on the stream which ran through the
hills. This was a much quicker and easier
way, and one which is common in Germany
and Switzerland. But, with all this help, the
father found it very hard to provide food and
fuel to make them all comfortable.

"At last poor Karl became so feeble that
he could no longer take care of the sheep.
For many weeks he was quite helpless with
rheumatism brought on by sitting out all day
in the damp air. Then it was that he found
the value of the little friends he had gained.

He had been a kind neighbor for years to
Terese's family, so the mother was willing to
work a little harder when he grew sick, that
her child might make up his bed and sweep
the cottage. One day she returned to her
home after having done this, and her mother
saw that she had been weeping. When she
asked the cause of her tears, Terese replied,
' Oh, mother dear, I can do nothing for Karl.
He has no wife to care for him, and no
children to toil for him as my father has.
Why did God not give *us* large flocks and
herds and vineyards ? Then I could do some
good, but now I can not. While I was at the
cottage this morning, Elise came in with a
servant carrying a large basket. When she
took out all the nice things and put them
on the little table I had just scoured, she
said, " I brought you these, Father Karl, because I love you." The old man kissed her
white hand and asked, " Why do you love
me, daughter ? " " Because you tell me such

beautiful stories about Willia_ Tell and Na-
poleon Bonaparte ; and I hope that these
good things will make you well, so that you
can tell me many more." Then he said, " I
thank you for your love, daughter, and I will
keep it in my heart, but I wish it were because I told you beautiful stories of *Christ*,
that you loved me." '

" ' I knew you would need me, dear mother,
so, as I was done, I came away while he was
talking so sweetly to Elise. She seemed impatient, and I am sure was not so well pleased
as she would have been with some other tale.'

" The mother did not seem to realize how
much Terese was really doing, any more than
did the child herself, but said, ' You must be
satisfied with the lot God has given you, my
good child.'

" The next day when her lowly duties were
all done, Terese went with the other children
to the old stone chapel to be catechized. The
aged pastor read the chapter in which Jesus,

to teach humility, washed the feet of his disciples, and said, ' If I then, your Lord and Master, have washed your feet, ye ought also to wash one another's feet. For I have given you an example that you should do as I have done to you.'

" Then the pastor told the little ones that any humble service, even this, which Christ performed for his disciples, would manifest our humility and willingness to serve him. 'God,' he said, ' does not need our service, for the cattle on a thousand hills are his, and he could feed and clothe all his poor without the aid of any one. But if you really love him, you will be watching for opportunities to show that love. Christ has laid aside his mortal body and gone to his glorious home on high. You can not bathe his aching head, — you can not remove his dust-soiled sandals, nor lave with water his weary feet, — you can not give him bread to eat or a place to lay his head. No, lambs of my fold, you can do none of these

things for the Redeemer in person, but you can
do all these and many more for those whom he
calls members of his body.   You can do it, —
you *have* done it.   Many of you have left your
sports and gone to speak kind words, and to
perform little kind acts to the godly old Karl.
I thank you, my lambs.   Jesus knows it, and
he will remember it in the great day, if you
did it from love to him.'

" After repeating their catechism, and joining
in prayer with the pastor, they went to their
homes.   At the door of the chapel Terese met
Elise, who said with a smiling face, ' Ah, you
see pastor Schmitz heard that I was at Karl's
yesterday ! '

" ' Yes,' said the good little Terese, who did
not envy her neighbor, ' he has no doubt
heard it.   It was very kind in you to leave
such a fine house, and go to that poor cottage,
and I thank you for it.'

" Now this dear child did not realize all this
time that she was doing far more for Father

Karl than was Elise. *She* would never have
crossed the hill alone to make his bed or scour
his floor or bring him water from the spring.
Ah, no! this was not the work for those white
hands. There were few on earth who strove
to bathe the Saviour's feet, but many who
sought to place a temporal crown upon his
head. Elise belonged to this latter class. She
could praise her aged fried, she could crown
his head with flowers, or send him gifts which
cost no self-denial; but the labor of Terese
was the same in character and prompted by
the same spirit as the washing of the disciples
and the anointing of the Saviour. Terese
understood what the good pastor had said, and
felt comforted. She called at the cottage on
her way, and repeated all she had heard to the
old man."

" Oh, what a sweet story that is, Auntie
dear," cried Jennie. " I could sit all night to
hear you talk ! "

"Auntie," said Ned, "these two stories are about *girls*. Won't you tell one about a boy to-morrow night?"

"Yes, my dear, I will," replied the kind Miss Thorne; "and after this, if you wish, I will tell a boy story every second evening. But remember, Ned, that this one applies to boys as well as to girls. You and your little friend can split wood or shovel a path for some poor widow, just as well as the girls can make a garment or watch beside a sick-bed. 'Where there's a will there's a way' to be useful; and children who walk with their eyes open will be sure to see work before them. If you stoop and pick up a stick or a stone which lies in the path of a lame or blind person, you do *a very little thing;* and yet Jesus will own it as an act done to himself, if your spirit is right in his sight."

CHAPTER V.

TALE-BEARING. — STORY OF BIRSEY, THE TATTLER.

"A boy's story to-night?" asked Aunt ιcy. "Well, gather up to the little fire this ιny evening; for, as it is summer now, we ιn't play winter any more. You have now idea of the old nursery, with its wood-fire d brass andirons. Bridget, not understand-ʒ our sport, asked your mother 'if Miss ιorne was striving to roast the children en-ely?'"

"I'm sure it has been cold enough for a fire ese three evenings," said Jennie.

"I wish we could have fires all summer," id Ned, "it makes the room so cheerful."

"I rather think you would not care for a e in August, my boy," said his mother.

"But now to our story."

BIRSEY, THE TATTLER.

" You know, my dears, the Word of God says, ' Thou shalt not go up and down as a tale-bearer among thy people.' ' The words of a tale-bearer are as wounds.'

" Tale-bearing, back-biting, and meddling in the affairs of others, are not reckoned by the world among gross sins. They are often looked upon only as acts of meanness, or impoliteness, or the result of ill-breeding. But the Scrip-tures speak plainly of these sins as hateful to God, and as provoking his displeasure against those who commit them. There can be no true sincerity in the character where these are a prevailing trait. Envy, jealousy, and hatred are the bitter fountains, whence these dark waters spring. The tale-bearer may flatter himself that he speaks only truth of his neighbors; but the bare truth will not long satisfy his growing desire for evil-speaking. Cruel hints and insinuations will next follow, till he separates very friends ; and after that will come deliberate falsehood, whereby the reputation of another may be wholly blasted. ' The words of the tale-bearer are as wounds.' Who ever loved a tale-bearer, a whisperer, or a busy-body in other men's matters ? Every one dreads his presence, and fears lest he himself be the next victim of his slanderous tongue.

" History has brought down to us through more than two long centuries the name of Birsey Smith ; but a most unenviable fame is his. Better far an honest oblivion ! From a boy, he had been shunned for his mischief-making propensities ; and of him it was true, in a most unfortunate sense, that ' the boy is father of the man.'

" He was a cobbler by trade, and worked around in the houses of the farmers ; although it was only as a matter of necessity that they employed him, so contemptible was his reputation in the little community where he dwelt.

" He lived in Scotland, in times of persecution, when the good and holy were cast into prison, or put to death for conscience' sake. A bounty was offered for the conviction or detection of any who worshiped God contrary to the established order. Smith, who was mean, covetous, and every way unlike what he should have been, professed, about this time, a great change of religious feeling, and desired to unite himself to the outcast band of disciples. With that charity which thinketh no evil, they opened their arms to receive him. For what, thought they, could induce a worldly man to seek a position with God's afflicted ones — to cast aside ease and safety, for poverty, persecution, and hatred ? Before this, no man on earth had loved him, unless it were *a mother*, of which history does not tell us ; and people who were forced to employ him set a double watch on their lips and guarded the words of their children while he was with them.

" Now ' Birsey,' as the boys scornfully called

Smith, knew the religious belief of all in the region, and the business of informer was becoming profitable. He must be able to swear to certain things considered disloyal, before he could 'receive the wages of unrighteousness.' This he could easily do, could he but gain admittance to the hearts of his employers. And with this dark purpose he crept into the trembling fold. He attended the secret meetings where, in darkness and fear, the lowly worshipers lifted up their hearts to God, or listened to the gospel of love and peace.

" After he had gathered sufficient for his purpose, he carried the information to the authorities, and many were cast into prison; while the name of the traitor remained a secret.

" At one time there was a meeting of those whose ' souls cried out after the Lord.' They felt themselves to be in a ' dry and thirsty land, where no water was;' and in their distress they remembered Him who smote the rock, and sent down manna from heaven. The

place where they met was so rocky and broker
that they felt secure from assault. And there
they sat as in a heavenly place in Christ Jesus
They 'sat under his shadow with great de
light,' fearing no evil.

"But suddenly a cry resounded through
the rocky glen. 'The troops! the troops!' I
was the voice of Smith which gave the alarm
and in a moment all was confusion and terror
Aged men, whose limbs could no longer bea
them swiftly, leaned on their staves, and
peered into the darkness for some hole or cave
in which to hide. Timid maidens flew unpro
tected, like frightened fawns, over the broad
moor. Mothers with their babes, and father
with their children, flew with almost super
natural haste to their lowly homes. The lately
rapt band were scattered in all directions; and
yet none ever saw the foe. No troops had
been in the region; and when Smith's false
report had scattered the assembly, he gathered
up the shawls, cloaks, bonnets, bibles and

psalm-books, which had been left in the flight, and bore them to his home as lawful booty.

"The eyes of the hunted Christians were now open, and they saw that a serpent had been cherished in their bosoms. He was despised more than ever by all the neighborhood, whatever their religious standing. Thenceforth he was a hissing and a by-word; for he had added to all his former crimes this Judas-like act against the oppressed Christians.

"Some time after this, he was engaged to work for a week at the farm-house of a godly man, named William Swan. He was anxious to begin his work very early on Monday morning; but the place was several miles distant from his house, and he knew the strictness with which this family regarded the sanctity of the Sabbath, and that they would censure him for performing his journey the night before. Smith was a great coward, and dared not take the walk before day on Monday. He firmly believed in ghosts, witches, and fairies, and to his guilty heart they all seemed spirits of evil. The breeze whispering through the thorn, or the ' caw, caw ' of an old crow from her home in the tree-top, made him frantic with terror.

" At length his deceitful heart brought relief. He decided to take holy time for his walk; and, as Swan would severely rebuke him if he should know it, to hide himself till daybreak, and then present himself there, panting, dusty, and weary, as if just from a long walk.

" Quite delighted with his own shrewdness, he went on, and arrived at the farm-house while Swan was engaged in his family devotions.

" The kitchen where they were seated was heated by a large fireplace in the center, whose huge chimney made its way through a great square opening overhead into a loft, and thence through the roof. Into this loft, smoky though it was, Birsey crept by an outside stair, and stretched himself, chilled and weary, near the chimney for the night.

After the devotions were over below, one of

the laborers remarked that they must be early astir next morning, as Smith was to be there. His name suggested a fruitful theme, and the children joined in expressing, in no gentle terms, their opinion of the mean and selfish man. Good William Swan caught a word of the scandal, and, raising his eye from his book, reproved the young backbiter, and bade him leave the sinful man in the hands of God, the righteous Judge. He warned the family not to call down the wrath of Heaven by speaking their own words or thinking their own thoughts on that holy day. The little ones meekly resumed their lessons in the catechism, and for half an hour the silence was unbroken.

"Then, all of a sudden, there fell upon the stone hearth — ring! ting! ting! — a shoemaker's knife! All laid down their books and gazed in mute astonishment at their father, who was no less confounded than they. But before there was time for a word, down came

an awl! — whence, no one saw. These were
the very implements used by the man against
whom they had been speaking. The affrighted
and superstitious laborers, ghastly pale, whispered that it was an omen for evil; for they
were sure that no such tools belonging to
mortals were ever left in the smoky loft overhead. They gazed upward into the awful
opening, when down came heavily what looked
like a man, but what they were sure was the
embodiment of all evil, — down into a bed of
burning coals!

"The family fled in terror; but the father,
stronger-hearted than they, ran to the rescue
of the mysterious visitor. Birsey was raked
from out the coals and ashes, with his clothes
burned and his hair singed close to his head.
He then confessed to the farmer how he had
hidden in the loft to conceal from him his Sab-
bath-breaking, and had heard all that was said
of him, until, overcome with heat and smoke,
he fell asleep. Turning round, he must have

dropped first his knife and awl and then him-self, into the fire. After a stern rebuke, he was pardoned and provided with more agree-able lodgings for the night.

"The end of this man, whose deceit and tale-bearing had been the means of shedding inno-cent blood, was truly awful. People at last feared to employ him, and he became an out-cast. His conscience scourged him on account of the fearful sins he had committed, and for a long time he was a vagabond on the earth. One day, his body was found suspended in an out-house belonging to William Swan — dead. No money could induce the workmen to bury him; and it was only done by a command of a neighboring earl to some of his own menials. They dug the suicide's grave on the boundary of two counties, a spot which was considered neutral ground. None wanted him laid in the quiet churchyard, where his dust would mingle with that of their loved and honored dead. William Swan tore down the building in which had been committed the fearful deed. The name of the wretched man is not even suffered to perish, but comes down to us, connected only with deceit, treachery and crime."

"Is that the end, Auntie?" asked Jennie.

"Certainly, my love; there could be no more after he was dead," replied Miss Thorne.

"Why," exclaimed Ned, "I never knew before that tattlers and busy-bodies were ever *men*. I thought all the gossips and mischief-makers were *women*."

"Well, Sir, you see your mistake; and I assure you there are a great many men mean enough nowadays to do just as poor, miserable Birsey Smith did, if they had the same temptation. A noble heart, whether in the breast of a man or a woman, will scorn a mean action. People often have such sins in their breasts, and do not know it themselves. We should pray, as David did, to God, — ' Cleanse thou me from secret faults.' "

CHAPTER VI.

" WELL, Master Ned," asked Aunt Lucy as she sat surrounded by the family and a few little friends on the piazza, " how would you like a blazing fire to-night ? "

Ned fanned away vigorously and replied, ' Not at all, Auntie; it was so raw and cold last night that I forgot how heat felt; but I know to-night ! "

" What is your story for this evening, Sister Lucy ? " asked Mr. Carrol. " I hope it is a very interesting one, for I have leisure to be a listener."

" Well, Sir," said Miss Thorne, laughing, ' it is a very small subject for so large a gentleman as you to hear about. I'm going to tell now about a *baby*."

THE BABY'S TOOTH.

" Some people think babies do no good in
the world, but only live here to torment those
who want to have quiet and order. But
think they are real little missionaries, making
others better by their smiles, and lifting heavy
loads of care off many hearts by their artless
ways.

" Well, years and years ago, when there
were few cars and when people had to jol
over shocking roads in great lumbering stage
coaches, the circumstance I am going to tel
took place. I can remember the time well
I assure you it was no holiday sport to g
' out West,' as people then called a good par
of New York State. It would not do for del
icate folks to travel then! There were very
few wedding tours. But of *this* journey!

" The evening coach was full — ' so full tha
it was an imposition on the passengers ' —
so said Miss Trimmer, who, with two or three

attern hats and a box of artificial flowers,
vas the last one to enter, notwithstanding the
nconvenience to which she put her fellow-
assengers.

" The village squire — never too amiable —
vas returning from court, where he had been
nonsuited in a case involving about a *fiftieth
part* of his estate ; of course, he was morose
and impatient. A worn-looking woman was
trying to quiet a restless baby by tossing it
up where there was not room to toss a bird,
because a simpering school-girl on the next
seat had whispered aloud to her *very* young
gallant, that ' babies were a perfect nuisance
in a stage-coach, and that she should think
any one would rather stay at home than travel
with one.' Poor, unfortunate baby ; poor,
sensitive, widowed mother ! Theirs was no
pleasure trip ; they were going, uncertain of
a welcome, to a rich relative of the newly
dead, the only one on earth of whom they
could ask aid. Comfort or pity the mother

did not look for. It was between these an
the surly squire that Miss Trimmer inserte(
herself. At the cruel remark of the incipien
belle, the widow turned her head to wip
away a tear, when her innocent half-yearlin;
grasped with her plump hand a huge buncl
of honeysuckles and carnation pinks whicl
dangled from the near side of Miss Trim
mer's bonnet.

" ' Will no one take pity on me ? ' shrieke(
the bearer of the flower burden. ' Will n(
gentleman shield me from such annoyances ?'

" ' Yes, Madam, *I* will,' answered an olc
gentleman who sat in a corner, resting hie
chin upon the ivory head of his cane. The
lady was soon safely installed in the seat
farthest removed from the vicious baby, and
the old man in her place. Now this cramped-
up child was a perfect democrat. She did not
know that she was poor and fatherless ; nor
that, when he lived, her father was only a
hard-working bricklayer. She knew nothing

all this, and seemed to think she had as
od a right to shout and crow as any other
by, and to pull flowers out of bonnets, too,
she could only reach them.   So at the new-
mer she went.   Her first effort was to se-
re his white beard, but that was immovable.
ie next reached out her hand for the seals,
d lastly grasped the cane.   ' Well, little
ch,' cried the dear old man, ' if you want
 get at my seals, you had better come a
tle nearer.'   So he took the willing baby
)m the weary mother and installed her on
s own knee.   The poor woman straightened
rself and drew a long breath, as if relieved
)m a burden she had not strength to bear.

" ' You look tired, Madam ; have you come
r to-day ? ' asked the merciful man.

" ' I've held the baby, Sir, thirty-six hours
 the cars before I got into the coach,' she
swered with a quivering lip.

" ' I don't see how any one can take care
 a tiresome baby,' again whispered the little

" ' Somebody held us all once, and took
care of us, too, my child,' replied the old
gentleman, whose ears were too keen to
lose her remark. ' Children must be taken
care of; they have their work to do, and
they generally do it faithfully.' And he
rattled his seals and key again for the happy child.

" The poor mother cast a look of unmin-
gled gratitude on her benefactor — yes, benefactor he was, though he had never given her
a crust nor a copper; for kind words are
often better than either. This good man alone,
of all the passengers — save the unconscious
baby — seemed at his ease.

" At length the horses stood still, and all
seemed pleased at the prospect of having the
company thinned. Miss Trimmer looked hope-
fully at the widow and baby, but they did not
move. An anxious, care-worn gentleman began to unwedge himself preparatory to alight-
ing. Then in the deepening twilight there

bounded from the dwelling, beside which the
coach had halted, a curly-headed boy of four
years. ' O Pa, Pa,' he shouted, as the pater-
nal head emerged from the coach-door, ' I've
good news for you ; you can't guess what has
happened to-day.' And clapping his chubby
hands and dancing for joy, he exclaimed, ' O
Papa, *the baby's got a tooth !* ' There was
a sudden revulsion of feeling in the coach.
The passengers all laughed heartily at the
vast importance of the news from that little
world, *home.* Miss Trimmer put her head out
of the coach-window and exclaimed, ' What a
darling little fellow ! ' The coachman forgot
to crack his whip for a whole minute as he
gazed at the happy boy. The father turned
round, smiled, raised his hat, and said ' good-
by ' to his fellow-travelers. The surly squire
laughed and drew home his feet, which had all
the way been stretched out on the widow's
territory, to her great inconvenience, saying,
' Beg your pardon, Ma'am.' Even Miss Trim.

mer was softened, for she opened the cover of
her reticule and gave the offending baby a
stick of candy, saying, ' Poor little thing, she
must have something to amuse her.'

" ' Well,' cried the laughing school-girl, ' I
do love children, after all — they are so funny
I can't help it ! '

" ' Never try to help it, child,' said the
baby's benefactor. ' They ought to be loved,
for they do a great deal for us grown folks.
Now don't you see that rosy boy, with the
news of the great acquisition to his family treasures, — a tooth for the baby, — has changed a
coach-full of anxious and ill-tempered people
into a cheerful and even kind-hearted company ? Don't you see how he has made
friends for my little companion here who is
too young to speak for herself ? Why, we
are all better now for riding with this little
one, and my word for it, you'll think of her
after you go home, too.' Then, turning to
the widow, he asked her to whose house she

was going. When she answered him, he said,
' Oh, it's too far to ride to-night with the poor
tired baby; stop and rest with us; grandmother will give even a strange baby a welcome, for we've just buried our pet at home,—
my daughter's little one. She made the house
very cheerful for us, but she's gone; but not
forgotten! No, I believe grandmother loves
all babies better since *she* died; so don't be
afraid of intruding.' Moved by such kindness,
the widow in an under-tone told her painful
errand to her new friend. ' Ah, ah!' he said,
' well, your relative is a kind man, if you go
at him just the right way, and folks say I
know how to manage him as well as any body.
In the morning I'll drive you over there, and
present your case in the most judicious manner. Never fear, he'll be kind to you; so
keep up good heart, my poor friend.'

" Overcome by such unlooked-for kindness,
she wept out the tears which had all day been
gathering in their fountain under the cold look

6

and sarcastic words of those around her. Miss
Trimmer, who, when not in a hurry or a crowd,
was really a kind-hearted woman, looked com-
passionately at the faint effort the young widow
had made toward wearing black for the dead.
' Won't you call at my shop with the lady, as
you go by in the morning, Mr. Bond?' she
asked; 'I should like to speak with her;'
and again she glanced at the straw hat with
its band of thin black ribbon, with an expression which promised a new one.

" ' Well, here we are, my friend,' cried the
old man, as the coach stopped before an old
brown mansion, ' and there is grandmother
in the door waiting for us.' The little belle
offered to hold the baby while the mother
alighted, and the softened squire handed out
her carpet-bag and basket. ' Good-night ' —
crack went the whip — and the cheerful trav-
elers rode on to their own homes. Light and
warmth and a cordial welcome for the night
and prosperity on the morrow awaited the

lonely widow, 'and all,' so said her noble
friend, 'because a baby had a tooth, and his
little brother told of it!'"

"When Jesus tells us, 'of such is the kingdom of heaven,' I'm quite willing to receive
his word," said Mr. Carrol; "for since we laid
our sweet little Johnnie in the grave, the hope
of seeing him there, still a baby, has added
new charms to heaven for me."

Mrs. Carrol wiped away a tear and said,
"Heaven has been sweeter to me also since
that day; and when I look sometimes at my
other children, so happy and so loving, it
almost breaks my heart to think that they
never saw and never loved the first lamb of
the fold. But in a moment I remember that
he is not lost to us, but resting for a season
in the bosom of the Good Shepherd. Then
I rejoice that when at last we shall be gathered in glory, he will be with us and one of
the dear little band. It is a holy thought,

' We have a baby in heaven ;' and let us all try to love Jesus that we may dwell for ever with him and the dear ones who wait for us there."

CHAPTER VII.

" It is *our* turn to-night, Auntie," said Ned, " to have a story — Joe's and mine. Do you know one about sailors ? "

" I don't know much about the sea, Ned, but I have known a good many who passed most of their lives on it," said Miss Thorne.

" Who ? " asked the boy.

" I had a lovely brother who would go from home as a sailor. He loved the very sound of the storm, and said the flapping of the canvas made him feel as if he must fly," replied the aunt.

" Which uncle is it ? " asked Jennie.

" Charlie, dear ; he died of yellow fever in a strange land, long before you were born.

But to-night let me tell you about our old neighbor and his grandson, who always looked on the bright side."

HUNTING FOR STARS.

" ' I KNEW we should have a storm,' said an aged man as he rose from his easy-chair and looked out upon the darkness. 'I told you so yesterday, Clara. When I see white caps off the beach I always think of the poor sailor on the coast. I don't like this coasting business at all, — there's twice the danger with half the profit of foreign voyages. I wish, Clara, you would consent to let Frank go to sea as he wants to ; I should feel less anxiety for him in a storm than I now do.'

" ' But you know, Father,' replied the lady, ' we see him so much oftener now, and I have so dreaded the open sea ever since his father was lost. It seemed so strange that no life but a sailor's would do for Frank ; my heart sinks at the thought of his making it his life business.'

" ' Not strange at all that he loves the sea,' replied the old man ; ' 'twas born in him, child ; and now, if I had my life to live over again, 1 would be nothing but a sailor.'

" ' Well, I suppose,' replied the lady, ' I must give up my will in the matter. He is a dear good boy, and I know it cost him a great struggle before he consented to compromise the matter by going in a coaster. I suppose I must spend my days looking for clouds and storms.'

" ' Oh, ho,' exclaimed the old man, rising and looking out again, ' a regular north-easter. But maybe they didn't sail on the seventeenth, Clara.   When I was among ships they used to say that a coaster might sail any day of the week but the one for which she was advertised. If they remained in port twenty-four hours after their time, they will not reach the rocks until the storm is over.'

" ' I hope,' said the mother, ' that God will protect him wherever he is, for thicker darkness

I never saw. But the wind has gone down since sunset, Father; it seems very calm now.'

"'Resting, perhaps, to blow with new fury,' said the old man, 'for it does not seem as if such a heavy storm could have passed over so soon. Let the boy go to India as he wants to, and take my word, Clara, when he's once off, a year's absence will not seem so long as a quarter does now. Why, child, when I was trading among the Islands, your mother used to get along alone for eighteen months at a time, and never complain.'

"'But, Father,' said the lady, 'mother was so cheerful and patient, always hoping and looking on the bright side; I often smile now as I think how she used to keep up her own courage and mine when you were gone. When the weather was fine, she used to say, "I've no doubt it is just as bright and calm where father is," — then when it stormed furiously she would say, "It is not at all likely this reaches out so far at sea as they must be now."' The old man laughed nervously, but in a moment he pressed his brow upon the ivory top of his staff, and wiped away the tears which fond old memories brought to his faded eyes.

" ' But, father, I haven't her strong trust to sustain me,' said the widow.

" ' No, child, no, you haven't, — you're more like me,' was the reply. 'Poor mother! she didn't make much stir in the world when she was here, but she left a wide place empty when she went away. It seems a lonely world to me since her head was laid low. Her gray hair was a crown of glory to her, but she wears a brighter crown now. Oh, Clara! I shall never cease thinking of her last night on earth, — the night of her triumph. When Frank came in so unexpectedly she looked so happy, and said, " I felt as if I should not be suffered to go till I had put my hand on that boy's head and blessed him." I said, " Now you are satisfied, are you not, mother ?" " No," she replied, " not yet, but I shall be when I awake in His likeness." She's satisfied *to-night*, Clara, while you and I sit here worrying about the boy she blessed.'

" ' It is wrong, father,' said the widow, as she saw the tears falling fast, ' it is wrong to distrust God in this way. Come, let's go into the sitting-room where there is a cheerful fire ; it always makes you feel lonely to sit by this dull stove.'

" ' I'm all broke to pieces, Clara,' said the old man rising, ' and sometimes I do wish Frank would stay on shore. There are so few left me now, that I think I should feel younger and stronger if I could have them around me.'

" ' I had strong hopes,' replied the lady, ' that Frank would grow up to be a companion for me and a useful man in the world. But his whole heart seems set on the billows and on wealth.'

" ' He may be a sailor and yet do much good,' said the old man. ' If he gets money, he may honor God with that.'

" ' He'll never hoard it up for himself,' said the mother, ' for he has your heart, father.'

" They entered the parlor and the old man sat down before the blazing fire, in the chair which his daughter had rolled in for him. He placed his cane in the corner of the fireplace, and was arranging the sticks to give a yet brighter light, when the widow exclaimed, ' Why, there is little Joe behind the window curtain! I thought you went to bed an hour ago, my boy.'

" ' I was on my way up-stairs, mother,' replied the boy, ' but I stopped here at the window a moment. Then I sat down in the window-seat to hunt for stars. You know the sky is so large, mother, that it took me a long time to look all over it.'

" The mother smiled at the simplicity of her child, but the grandfather said, ' You will look a long time, Joe, before you find a star in this dark sky.'

" ' Why, dear Grandpa,' said the boy earnestly, ' I found *one* some time ago, and now I see another. A heavy cloud has just broken and now the stars are beginning to peep through.' The old man looked incredulous. He rose, and standing by the boy, looked out, and said, ' I don't see a single star, Joe.'

" ' That's because you have not looked long enough, Grandpa ; fix your eye up there,' he said, pointing to the broken cloud, ' and if you wait a moment, you'll see stars. They look pale, but they'll soon be brighter, for the cloud is moving away from them.'

" ' I see them now, Joe, my darling,' exclaimed the old man, laying his hand fondly on the curly head. ' Come here, Clara, and see if God can not scatter the cloud which shadows Frank's pathway home.

> " Ye fearful saints, fresh courage take ;
>   The clouds ye so much dread,
> Are big with mercy, and shall break
>   In blessings on your head."

" ' But tell me, my boy, what made you

think of hunting for stars amid the thick darkness ? '

" ' I noticed, Sir,' said the child, ' that ever since we have been expecting Frank home, you and mother have been all the time looking for clouds and storm. So, after the rain and wind came, I thought I would look for starlight, and perhaps that would come too ; I always find when I want any good thing and look patiently for it, I am sure to find it.'

" ' Hear that, Clara ? ' said the old man. ' Doesn't that sound just like your mother ? '

" And the clouds broke and flew away, the rain ceased and the winds were hushed.

" It was a cheerful little group which gathered round the sparkling fire the next evening. How joyfully both grandfather and mother gazed into the hopeful face of Frank, as he told how, amid the wind and darkness of the previous night, they had striven to keep off from the rocky coast, and how rejoiced they were when, contrary to all weather-signs, the wind ceased blowing and the stars came out to guide them to their desired haven. How joyfully did the brave boy listen to the story of little Joe hunting for the stars for his dear sake! How patiently did he hear his mother's warning not to set his heart on this world, and her expressions of fear for his future life. When she spoke of her hopes and prayers over his cradle, that he might grow up to love God, and to serve him as a minister or a missionary, he replied ' But, dearest mother, all the good men must not be missionaries ; some must make money to sustain those who preach the gospel. I will try to be one of this class ; but to sea I must go ! I cannot breathe freely on shore more than a month at a time.'

" ' Just as I felt when I was young,' said the old man. ' You must let him go to India once, Clara. Who can tell but God may make him a blessing there.'

" ' Oh, Mother,' said the boy, ' I long to go abroad, but I never will without your consent.'

" The fond heart of the old man ceased not to beat till he had welcomed Frank again and again from foreign lands; till he had seen his ambition chastened, and gold sought for a nobler purpose than to gratify the pride of life. And when he slept in the dust, the widow was spared to see her mother's blessing fall upon her first-born. She lived to know that her early prayers for him were answered; that, although not a minister of the gospel, he was doing a work which no Christian at home can do for his brother in heathen lands, and what no missionary can do for his fellow-laborer. When abroad he held up the drooping hands of God's servants to the Gentiles; on the sea he was the honored instrument of cheering the fainting heart, of supporting the aching head, and of holding to the parched lips of the missionary the cup of cold water, for Christ's sake. Many the fears he quelled, many the tears he wiped away, many the acts of love which none but a Christian seaman could perform, registered beneath his name on high, when his mother was no more.

" Surely light arose to that mother in her darkness, and even while she, distrustfully, was looking for clouds and tempest, the God of the widow and the Father of the fatherless was removing everything which prevented the stars from lighting her darkness.

> " 'Judge not the Lord by feeble sense,
> But trust him for his grace ;
> Behind a frowning providence
> He hides a smiling face.' "

CHAPTER VIII.

BITTER WORDS.—THE STORY OF LITTLE KITTY.

"SATURDAY night come so soon!" exclaimed Aunt Lucy, as the little group gathered round her in the parlor. "'Another six days' work is done;' I wonder what messages all these seconds and minutes and hours and days have borne to heaven! What have we done to make ourselves better and others happier? Have we overcome any sin which has been lurking in our hearts; or have we cherished all these, and committed new ones? Are we nearer heaven, dear little ones, or farther from it than we were last Saturday night? When we go away alone, let us ask our hearts these questions, and pray God for grace to live to him. The story I have for you to-night will teach you to treat each other from day to day

7

just as if each was to be your last meeting together; so that, should death come suddenly to any one of you, you will have no guilt on your conscience, for having spoken harshly or acted cruelly to those whose pardon you can not ask."

"I often wish," said Mrs. Carrol, "that I could recall a few harsh words I once said to a poor girl, who lived as a domestic with my mother when I was not older than Ned. She was apt to be very fretful, and used to scold when we touched any thing in the kitchen. I one day heard my mother say she could not keep her on this account; so, going into the kitchen, and meeting with the usual treatment, I said in a passion, 'Scold away, old Margery Pool, as fast as you can, or else you won't get through before you go.'

"'Go where?' asked the girl in surprise.

"'Home to your father's; my mother says you sha'n't stay here and scold her children any longer. I hope you'll go as quick as you can, for we are all sick of the sight of you.'

" I never shall forget," continued Mrs. Carrol, " the look of utter despair with which she threw her blue apron over her face and sank into a chair. Then she sobbed out, ' Nobody knows how hard I try to do right; but half the time I'm too sick to work at all. Your mother *will* have all right in the kitchen, and when you come in and clatter it up when I am too tired to go over it again, I can't help scolding. Oh, dear! it's a poor home I've got to go to — it's a drunkard's home ; and, more than that, mother's looking for my wages to buy winter clothes for the children.'

" When tea was over that evening, we called and rang the bell, but Margery was nowhere to be found. She had taken her little paper-covered trunk in her arms, and walked away four miles to her miserable home in a forlorn neighborhood. I felt very guilty, and told my mother what I had said. She blamed me very much, and said, ' I, who was a happy child, ought to be more tender of the feelings of the poor; and that she should ride over to Pine Hollow, to give Margery her wages, and should insist on my going with her to ask her pardon.' But before the time came, Margery's mother walked over for the money. She said her girl was very sick, and kept repeating all the time, ' Oh, Mother, I tried so hard to help you! I shall never scold any more.' And the poor thing died with a fever which had been hanging about her for weeks. I prayed God to forgive my cruelty, and I hope he has done so; but to this day it is a blot on my memory, which I would give a great deal to wash away. But, Lucy, dear, the children are waiting for your story, so I will detain you no longer."

" It will be much the same as yours, only this is of a little sister, instead of a servant. I well remember the time when Margery left us. Mother took us to the funeral, that we might see a drunkard's home, and learn to feel for the little children there. Oh, what desolation was there! The old man sat with his hands over his eyes, as if ashamed to look any one in the face; and well he might be, for the dead girl wore her life out trying to feed him in idleness, and to keep the family from starvation. My story to-night is about a little girl I knew in my youth."

LITTLE KITTY.

" LITTLE Kitty was a bright, merry, and affectionate girl of fourteen. She was ever ready to oblige, and being the child of an invalid mother and the sister of two gay and fashionable young ladies, she never lacked for opportunity to exercise this amiable quality. She was the helper of every-body, from the sick mother down to the cook. The mother called on her because she came with a step so soft and a voice so gentle, — the sisters, because no one could arrange their hair and assist at

their toilet so tastefully as the graceful Kitty,
— the cook, not only because it saved her
' many a weary foot's-length, but for the comfort o' seein' how like a born lady she'd stoop
to assist the poor bodies benathe her.' At any
rate, Kitty found business enough to weary
many a foot less light, and to discourage many
a heart less kind and willing than hers. She
ran on all her sisters' errands, carrying flowers,
books, and notes to their friends, ' because she
did it so prettily, and servants were *so stupid*.'
She was a school-girl, and if ever she ventured
to hint that her lessons must be learned, they
said, ' Oh, what of that, Kitty ? You are so
smart that you can do all that after we are
gone, in the evening.'

" And so she did, for many a long winter's
night studying and sleeping alternately in her
chair, and keeping a light and a warm fire for
the revelers. And then when they were warm
enough to speak, Kitty darling must pull down
all the finery she had so lately erected, and

listen, for her reward, to an account of the splendid assembly, and to promises of going with them in two or three years.

" ' I wonder what you'll do for a dressing-maid *then?* ' Kitty would ask with an arch smile ; and then, with a fond kiss from each, she would slip off to her mother's disturbed bed, there to dream of fractions, verbs, artificial flowers, and cameo bracelets, all engulfed for ever in her mother's gruel porringer !

" The girls had long been prevented from reciprocating the invitations of their gay friends, and as the winter wore away and no alarming symptoms appeared in the case of their mother, they decided to give a little entertainment. No objections were made by the invalid, for she felt that the house had been made gloomy long months by her illness, and was willing to endure some annoyance, could she but make her fatherless children happy.

" When the evening arrived and the all·

important work of the toilet began, it was
found out that the florist had failed to send
the bouquets. *No flowers for their hair,—
what could they possibly do!* The servants
were too busy to be spared, so of course
'Kitty would *have* to go.' And she went,
not **very** cheerfully, we must say. For once
a tear came to her eye, as she looked out
into the darkening street, upon the cold snowy
pavement.

"' Can't you do without them ? ' she asked.

"' Do without them ? Why, Kitty, that does
not sound like you,' replied one of her sisters.

"' Well, girls, the truth is,' exclaimed Kitty,
' I am so weary that I can hardly stand now ;
I'm sure you do not realize how much I have
done to-day, or you would not ask me to go.'

" The sisters both looked wounded at this un-
expected remark, and the eldest said reproach-
fully, ' Well, we can go without the flowers, if
you are so *disobliging.*' Her better nature
rebuked her before the words were off her

lips, but she was vexed and would not say so.

"'Here then, Kitty,' said the second one, 'is my pearl flower for your hair, — you see I am willing to gratify you — even when you are selfish.'

"Kitty burst into tears, and darted from the room. She knew that she was not selfish, and the accusation went like an arrow to her heart. Her sisters, too, felt unhappy; not so much that they must dress without the flowers, as because they knew they had been unjust and cruel to the being whom, of all others on earth, they most tenderly loved. One bade the other go to Kitty's room and tell her they did not mean what they had said, but neither went for some time, and then she was not there. What was their surprise, in less than an hour, to see her enter their chamber with swollen eyes, but smiling lips, bearing the flowers! With shame, they thanked the weary child, but in the excitement and bustle, they

did not kiss her, they did not ask pardon for
their heartless cruelty. Oh, how does worldly
vanity harden the heart of the naturally good
and loving !

" The guests were gone, the lights extin·
guished, and the weary girls, after assuring
themselves that their mother had been in no
way injured by the noise, sought their pillows,
saying, as they kissed her tenderly, ' Good-
night, dear Mother, Kitty will be up in a
moment.'

" Long after all save the sick one had been
lost in slumber, a ringing from her chamber
brought down her daughters. ' Why, my children, where can Kitty be ? It is more than
an hour since you left me, and no sound have
I heard in the house.' The servants were
roused, and all descending together sought the
child. Then the sisters remembered that they
saw nothing of her after the guests began to
arrive. On reaching the front basement, there
in the cold and darkness lay Kitty, robed only

in a thin muslin, sleeping the heavy deep slumber of one over-wearied and ill. They strove to rouse her, but could only get her enough awake to say, ' Oh, don't, don't, — I'm so weary that I can not go! Oh, I've tried, but can not walk, — wait till our own flowers grow! I am not selfish, do not call me so, — I am sick and tired, but not selfish. Oh, I'm so weary, let me sleep, sisters ! '

" The girls wept bitterly as poor fond Nora with loud lamentations carried the sick child up-stairs in her arms. The three watched over her, all wearied as they were, while another strove to calm the mother's fears. No effort could avail to warm the shivering form until morning began to break. Then the cold, blue lip and cheek changed their hue to burning red. Kitty knew no one around her, answered none of their questions, but only murmured, ' No, no ! Ask my mother if I have been an unfeeling, selfish child ! ' In the morning, while the doctor was in the sick-room, the florist called to apologize for his young man's carelessness. 'I hope,' he said, 'the young lady did not take cold last night. I noticed that while at the store waiting for the bouquets she tried to dry her feet; but her shoes were full of snow and water. She seemed very weary and asked for a seat, poor child! I felt troubled lest she might be made ill through our neglect, and could not rest till I had inquired.'

"Kitty was indeed very ill, but conscience told her sisters in words not to be misunderstood that others than he were to blame; that their heartlessness had brought on the fever which might consume her sweet life away.

"The burning heat soon seized the brain of the dear child, and no skill had power to allay it, no love had strength to awaken her to a sense of her condition. She still moaned piteously in her troubled dreams, 'Kiss me, sisters, and say you will forgive me; then I'll go out in the night and the storm and bring your flowers. Oh, how cold the white flowers are; they are made of ice, — cold, cold! The red

flowers burn my fingers, but I will bring them!
I am not selfish, am I, Mother? Oh dear!'

" Kitty died, and what then were balls and
parties and tinsel and flowers to her agonized
sisters! They wept bitterly over her coffin;
but the flowers with which their love had filled
it, and which should have been messengers of
hope and peace, were as daggers to their
hearts, reminding them of the night she went
sick and weary to procure the like to deck
them for the revel. They robed themselves
in deepest weeds of woe; they extolled her
virtues; they enshrined her image in their
hearts; they erected a costly monument to
her memory; but they could never satisfy
their own hearts, never repay poor, sweet
Kitty for those hours of sorrow, nor take
back again those bitter words.

" Dear, dear children," said Aunt Lucy,
" keep your hearts pure from such sins towards each other; for you little know at what

time the Son of man will call for you or for those with whom you associate from day to day. If either of you has wronged or wounded any person, go at once and ask forgiveness, so that there will be nothing of that kind left undone, should death come suddenly. If God spares you to old age you will be better men and women for thus crucifying your pride now. Pray that God will help you to set a watch on your lips that you sin not with your tongue. The lips are the door of the heart; so all can tell what is within, by what passes through them. Now good-night, away to your prayers and your slumbers. God bless you, my darlings."

" Shall you tell us a Sunday-night story, Auntie?" asked Jennie.

"Perhaps I will; but now, dears, go to bed, and I will tell you in the morning what seems best to be done to-morrow night."

THE END.

CHOICE
Sunday-School Books.

GRANDMOTHER MERWIN'S HEIRESS. Mrs. M. F. Butts. 'mo. 308 pp. 6 cuts. $1 25.

FRONTIER AND CITY. Miss A. L. Rouse. 12mo. 294 pp. cuts. $1 25.

THE WHATSOEVER TEN. Minnie E. Kenney. 12mo. 295 pp. cuts. $1 25.

JUDGE HAVERSHAM'S WILL. Miss I. T. Hopkins. 12mo. .1 pp. 4 cuts. $1 25.
The young hero will be admired for his sterling manly qualities.

MARGIE AT THE HARBOR-LIGHT. Rev. E. A. Rand. 12mo. cuts. 264 pp. $1.

CHANGING PLACES; or, How One Boy Climbed Up and nother Slipped Down. Miss C. M. Trowbridge. 12mo. 217 pp. cuts. Cloth, 90 cts.

BERNIE'S LIGHT. Minnie E. Kenney. 12mo. 272 pp. 4 cuts. loth, $1 10.

ARROW HEAD LIGHT. Miss I. T. Hopkins. 12mo. 366 pp. loth, $1 25.

MRS. MORSE'S GIRLS. Minnie E. Kenney. 12mo. 282 pp. loth, $1.

ROGER DUNHAM'S CHOICE. Jennie Harrison. 12mo. 270 pp. loth, $1.

TALL CHESTNUTS OF VANDYKE. Miss I. T. Hopki
12mo. 395 pp. 5 cuts. $1 50.

DUNCAN KENNEDY'S NEW HOME. Mrs. L. L. Rouse. 12i
324 pp. 4 cuts. $1 25.

HOPE REED'S UPPER WINDOWS. Howe Benning. 12i
304 pp. 4 cuts. $1 25.

DICK LANGDON'S CAREER. Mrs. S. A. F. Herbert. 12i
248 pp. 4 cuts. $1.

FROLIC BOOKS. Mrs. M. F. Butts. 6 vols. 16mo. $4 25 per i

**FOXWOOD BOYS AT SCHOOL; or, More Doings of t
McDonogh Boys.** Mrs. E. P. Allan. 12mo. 267 pp. $1.

HER CHRISTMAS AND HER EASTER. Rev. E. A. Ra
12mo. 187 pp. $1.

HARRY'S TRIP TO THE ORIENT. Rev. Charles S. Newb
12mo. 344 pp. 22 cuts. $1 50.

JEAN MACDONALD'S WORK. 12mo. 384 pp. 6 cuts. $1

JUST IN TIME. Mrs. Reaney. 12mo. 374 pp. 4 cuts. $1 25.

URSULA'S BEGINNINGS. 12mo. 296 pp. 4 cuts. $1 25.

HARD TO WIN. Mrs. G. Cupples. 12mo. 158 pp. 4 cuts. 75

THE GOOD-TIMES GIRLS. Miss I. T. Hopkins. 12mo. 472
6 cuts. $1 50.

HAMPERED. Mrs. A. K. Dunning. 12mo. 198 pp. 3 cuts. 90

HONEST WULLIE. Mrs. L. L. Rouse. 12mo. 316 pp. 5 cuts. $1

SEVENTEEN AND TWICE SEVENTEEN. Mrs. A. F. I
fensperger. 12mo. 320 pp. 4 cuts. $1 25.

VACATION DAYS AT FOXWOOD. Mrs. E. P. Allan. 12i
224 pp. 4 cuts. $1.

CLUNY MACPHERSON. Mrs. Amelia E. Barr. 12mo. 311 pp. cuts. $1 25.

DAISY SNOWFLAKE'S SECRET. Mrs. G. S. Reaney. 12mo. 3 pp. 6 cuts. $1 25.

FINDING HER PLACE. Howe Benning. 12mo. 368 pp. 5 cuts. . 50.

UP TO THE MARK. Miss I. T. Hopkins. 12mo. 372 pp. 4 cuts. . 50.

QUIET CORNERS. Howe Benning. 12mo. 373 pp. 4 cuts. $1 50.

TARRYPORT SCHOOL-GIRLS. A. L. Noble. 16mo. 272 pp. cuts. $1.

VICTORY AT LAST. Miss C. M. Trowbridge. 12mo. 232 pp. cuts. $1.

MADGE MARLAND. Laura Francis. 12mo. 320 pp. 4 cuts. $1 25.

OPENING PLAIN PATHS. Howe Benning. 12mo. 336 pp. cuts. $1 25.

READY AND WILLING. Miss I. T. Hopkins. 12mo. 333 pp. cuts. $1 25.

THEO AND HUGO. Mary B. Wyllys. 16mo. 320 pp. 4 cuts. $1.

THE BLUE-BADGE BOYS. Miss I. T. Hopkins. 16mo. 384 pp. cuts. $1 25.

FATHER'S HOUSE. Howe Benning. 16mo. 278 pp. 4 cuts. $1.

NELLIE'S NEW YEAR. Rev. E. A. Rand. 16mo. 351 pp. cuts. $1 10.

CHRISTMAS JACK. Rev. E. A. Rand. 16mo. 231 pp. 6 cuts. $1.

Model Libraries.

EACH IN A CHESTNUT CASE.

— ◆ —

MODEL LIBRARY, No. 1.

For older scholars. 50 vols. 16mo. NET, $20.

MODEL LIBRARY. No. 2.

For intermediate scholars. 18mo. 50 vols. NET, $15.

MODEL LIBRARY, No. 3.

For older scholars. 16mo. 50 vols. NET, $25.

MODEL LIBRARY, No. 4.

For the Infant Class, 18mo. 50 vols. NET, $10.

MODEL LIBRARY, No. 5.

For older scholars. 25 vols. 16mo. NET, $15.

STAR LIBRARY.

One hundred volumes. 18mo. See last page.

MISSIONARY LIBRARY.

Twelve volumes. Only $10 NET. See next page.

Top shelf:

KESA AND SAIJIRO — MISSIONARY LIBRARY

GLIMPSES OF MAORI LAND — MISSIONARY LIBRARY

EVERY-DAY LIFE IN INDIA — MISSIONARY LIBRARY

LIFE AND ADVENTURE IN JAPAN — MISSIONARY LIBRARY

FROM HONG-KONG TO THE HIMALAYAS — MISSIONARY LIBRARY

ALONG RIVER AND ROAD IN FUH-KIEN — MISSIONARY LIBRARY

Bottom shelf:

JOTTINGS FROM THE PACIFIC — MISSIONARY LIBRARY

HOME-LIFE IN CHINA — MISSIONARY LIBRARY

AMONG THE MONGOLS — MISSIONARY LIBRARY

MADAGASCAR AND FRANCE — MISSIONARY LIBRARY

SCENES IN SOUTHERN INDIA — MISSIONARY LIBRARY

OLD HIGHWAYS IN CHINA — MISSIONARY LIBRARY

POPULAR SERIES.

BOOKS IN STOUT PAPER COVERS.

Those marked thus (‡) are illustrated.

	PRICE.		PRI
Advice to Young Christians	10	Easy Lessons‡	
Alice Maitland's Trial‡	10	Ethel Seymour‡	
Alone in London.‡ Stretton	15	Eve and her Daughters‡	
Amusements, in the Light of Reason. Haydn	15	Evidences of Divine Revelation. Spencer	
Amy's New Home‡	10	Fall of Jerusalem‡	
An Irish Heart.‡ *Temperance Tales*	10	Fisherman's Boy‡	
Annals of the Poor.‡ Legh Richmond	20	Frank Merton's Conquest‡	
Antonio Bishallany	15	Fritz Hazell.‡ *Temperance Tales*	
Anxious Inquirer. James	15	George Wayland‡	
As a Medicine.‡ *Temperance Tales*	10	Gospels Written, When Were Our. Tischendorf	
Atonement, Discourses on	10	Grace Abbott‡	
Bartimeus of the Sandwich Islands	5	Groggy Harbor.‡ *Temperance Tales*	
Basil, or Honesty and Industry‡	10	Hammond, Capt. M. M.	
Benny‡	5	Happy Fireside‡	
Bertha Alston‡	10	Harry the Whaler‡	
Bertie's Fall‡	10	Herbert: True Charity.‡ *Ministering Children*	
Bessie Kirkland‡	10	Historical Tales for Young Protestants‡	
Bethlehem and her Children‡	10		
Bible Reader's Help	20	Holiday Pictures.‡ 48 pictures	
Blanche Gamond‡	10	Horace Carleton's Essay‡	
Blood of Jesus. Reid	10	How to Answer Objections to Revealed Religion	
Bloom of Youth‡	10		
Bud of Promise, etc.‡	10	Huguenots, etc., The‡	
Buster and Baby Jim‡	10	Jessica's First Prayer.‡ Stretton	
Caroline Morin‡	5	Joe and Sally‡	
Charles Atwell, etc.‡	10	Joe Blake's Temptation‡	
Chinese Coast, etc.‡	10	John the Baptist	
Christianity's Challenge. Herrick Johnson, D. D. 16mo	25	Joseph and his Brethren‡	
		Judson, J. C., etc.‡	
Christian Queen, etc.‡	10	Kitty Grafton.‡ *Temperance Tales*	
Christie's Old Organ.‡ Walton	15	Life Preserver.‡ *Temperance Tales*	
Cinnamon-Isle Boy‡	15	Lilian ‡	
Concert Programme‡	10	Little Bessie, etc.‡	
Daniel, Life of‡	15	Little Captain.‡ Peebles	
David Acheson, etc.‡	10	Little Dot, and Angel's Christmas.‡ Walton	
Davidson, E., etc.‡	10		
Deserted Heroine, The‡	5		
Dora Felton's Visit‡	10	Little Gold Keys‡	

WALL ROLLS.

THOUGHTS FOR THE DAY. A Wall Roll with Scriptural and poetical selections in harmony with a leading thought for each day. With suggested Bible readings for the year. Mounted on walnut roller. 32 pp. 75 cts.

LIGHT ON LIFE'S PATH. A selection of passages for every day the month, with a leading text. Elegant, large type, and black walnut ller. 32 pp. 75 cts.

MORNING SUNBEAMS. Selected by Mrs. Prentiss for daily use. ιrge Roll same as the above. Large, clear type, easy to read across the om. 32 pp. 75 cts.

PICTORIAL WALL ROLL. A choice full-page picture on each ιge, with a few lines of suggestive explanation. Pictures tell a whole ɔry without a word. Mounted on walnut roller. Size, 13 by 20 inches. pp. 75 cts.

LEAD ME TO THE ROCK THAT IS HIGHER THAN I. Psa. 61:2.

Who is a rock save our God? Psa. 18:31.

For thou hast been a shelter for me, and a strong tower from the enemy. Psa. 61:3.

For thou hast been a strength to the needy in his distress, a refuge from the storm, a shadow from the heat. Isa. 25:4.

And the peace of God, which passeth all understanding, shall keep your hearts and minds through Christ Jesus. Phil. 4:7.

BIBLE HELPS.

Dictionary of the Bible. Revised edition. Over 200,000 sol' 360 illustrations, 18 maps. 720 pp. 8vo. Cloth, $2; sheep, $2 50; morocc $3 50; Levant, $5.

Cruden's Concordance. 561 pp. 8vo. Cloth, $1; sheep, $2 25.

Bible Text-Book. A topical concordance, with maps, indexe chronologies, and tables of various kinds. 232 pp. 12mo. Cloth, 90 cts.

Hanna's Life of Christ. 20 engravings. Cloth, $1 50.

Stalker's Life of Paul. With map. Cloth, 60 cts.

Stalker's Life of Christ. Cloth, 60 cts.

Schaff's Through Bible Lands. 31 maps and illustration Cloth, $2 25.

Studies in Mark's Gospel. Rev. C. S. Robinson, D. D. 12m Cloth, $1 25; paper, 50 cts.

From Samuel to Solomon. Rev. C. S. Robinson, D. D. 12m Cloth, $1 25; paper, 50 cts.

Barrows' Sacred Geography. Cloth, $2 25.

Barrows' Companion to the Bible. Cloth, $1 75.

Gage's Studies in Bible Lands. 60 illustrations, 12 map Cloth, $1 25.

Howson's Scenes from the Life of St. Paul. Illustrate Cloth, $1.

Gosse's Sacred Streams. 44 engravings and a map. Cloth, $1 2

Schauffler's Meditations on the Last Days of Chris Cloth, $1 50.

Locke's Commonplace-Book of the Holy Bible. Cloth, $1

Bible Reader's Help. With two maps. A good book for Sabbat schools, as a small Bible Dictionary. Cloth, 40 cts.; paper, 20 cts.

Pocket Concordance. A new compilation. Cloth, 60 cts.; m rocco, limp, $1 25 NET.

Bible Atlas and Gazetteer. Super-royal octavo. 32 pp. S fine large maps, a full list of all the geographical names in Scripture, wit a valuable series of tables. Cloth, $1 25.

Teacher's Bibles.

NEW MINION " TYPE, 6¾ inches long, 5 ins. wide, 1¾ ins. thick. References between the verses. **This is the book so highly recommended by Ralph Wells, of New York, and others.**

    Morocco, leather-lined, round corners, gilt edges --- ----------- $3 50
        For Text-Book Edition, order No. 184.
        For Concordance Edition, order No. 214.

    Levant, kid-lined, silk-sewed, round corners, red under gold
        edges, with pocket -- 5 00
        For Text-Book Edition, order No. 185.
        For Concordance Edition, order No. 215.

LARGE PRINT" EDITION, 7½ ins. long, 5¼ ins. wide, 1¾ ins. thick. References in centre of page.

    Turkey morocco, limp or stiff -------------------------------- 4 00
    Levant morocco, kid-lined, full-flexible, silk-sewed, protecting
        edges, round corners, with pocket ------------------------ 10 00
    Same as above, but containing the Bible Text-Book and Con-
        cordance, together with all the other helps found in both
        editions. No. 227 -------------------------------------- 11 00

ARGE PAPER (Wide Margin) EDITION, 8½ ins. long, 6 ins. wide, 1⅞ ins. thick. References in centre of page. With inch margin and 24 blank pages for notes, Scripture Index, New Maps, etc.

    Levant morocco, kid-lined, full-flexible, silk-sewed, protecting
        edges, round corners, with pocket. No. 199---------------- 11 00

ARGE PAPER (Wide Margin) EDITION. The above book, with Bible Text-Book instead of the Scripture Index, everything else being the same.

    Levant morocco, kid-lined, silk-sewed, protecting edges, with
        pocket, round corners. No. 201 ------------------------ 12 00

BIBLE STUDENT'S EDITIONS. Full-faced **Bourgeois** type, three sizes larger than Bagster's largest 8vo, with Bible Student's Manual, comprising Chronological Index, Maps, Charts, Harmonies, etc. 8½ ins. long, 6 ins. wide, 1⅞ thick.

    Levant morocco, or Sealskin, kid-lined, silk-sewed, full-flexible,
        with pocket, round corners. **Order No. 250**----------- -- 10 00

    The same book containing **in addition** to the above matter
        our revised Bible Text-Book. **Order No. 255**----------- 11 00

Bibles *and* Testaments

FAMILY BIBLE, with Notes and Instructions. Size, 11½ by 9½, and 3 inches thick. This valuable edition of the Bible has been issue in a new form, making it a most convenient book for family use.

The Notes and Explanations are concise, and at the same time give th results of the best study; and the authors had no theory to establish, bu simply to show what is the mind of the Spirit regarding the Word.

It contains Explanatory Notes and Practical Instructions by Rev. Justi Edwards, D. D., revised by Prof. E. P. Barrows.

Roan, panelled sides, gold stamp, sprinkled or marbled edge---- $6 0
Persian morocco, panelled sides, gilt edge--------------------- 7 5
Turkey   "   "   "   --------------------- 12 0
Levant   "   bevelled boards, tooled sides, sewed full-flexible 14 0

A NEW CHEAP EDITION. Prepared expressly for this valuabl work at a price that will come within the reach of all. It contains, beside the Harmony of the Gospels, Chronology, Maps, Tables of Weights an Measures, and Family Record, eight elegant illustrations, and is strongl bound.

Roan, blank side stamp, sprinkled edge ---------------------- $4 0

NEW TESTAMENT AND PSALMS. These portions of th Family Bible, with Notes, Maps, Tables, etc., are published separately in handsome royal octavo volume of 524 pp. Size, 7¾ by 11 ins., ¾ in. thick.

Cloth, $1 75; cloth gilt, $2 50; sheep, $3.

THE POCKET BIBLE. Three volumes with Notes, Instruction: Maps, and Tables. 2,676 pp. Small 12mo. Size, per set, 4½ ins. wide, 6¾ ins. long, 3¾ ins. thick. This edition contains all the notes and instruction that are in the large edition, and will do much to popularize and increas the usefulness of this invaluable work.

Three volumes, cloth, $3.

THE POCKET TESTAMENT. Over 175,000 circulated. Th New Testament is also printed in a neat and complete small 12mo editior for the use of young people, Sabbath-schools, etc. With Maps, Harmony o the Gospels, Chronologies, etc. 810 pp. Size, 5 by 7 inches.

Cloth, $1; cloth gilt, $1 40; sheep, $1 50.

Sunday-School Cards.

CTS.

A B C Picture Cards. 28 in a packet. 4½ by 3¼ inches ------ 20

A Card of the Ten Commandments. In clear type. 5½ by 3½ ins. -- 1

Alphabet Card. With Lord's Prayer and Commandments in verse. 5½ by 3½ ins. ---------------------------------- 1

Bible Cards. 96 in a packet, each with a short text and colored printed border. 2¼ by 1½ ins. ------------------ 15

Bible Flowers. A choice packet of the flowers of the Holy Land, painted from nature by MISS BIRD. 12 cards with different texts. 3 by 5 ins. --- 20

Bible Words. 144 cards in bright colors, with different texts--- 25

Children of the Year. 12 fine cards with easel backs to stand upon table, with ideal heads, by MISS LATHBURY, illustrating the seasons, with carefully selected texts. 4¼ by 5½ ins. -- 25

Faithful Sayings. 12 floral cards with texts. NET----------- 12

Floral Texts, B. 96 cards. 2¼ by 1½ ins. -------------------- 20

Floral Texts, C. 144 cards. 1¾ by 1½ ins. .... --------------- 25

Gems from the Psalms. A selection of 72 texts from the Psalms, in colors. 3¼ by 2¼ ins-------------------------- 20

Gift Cards for Children. In colors, on nice cardboard. 72 in a packet. 4 by 2¼ ins. ----------------------------------- 20

Gospel Words. 12 floral cards, with choice texts, all bearing the "Good News." 2½ by 4¼ ins. -------------------------- 15

Gracious Invitations. Floral cards, copyright designs. 12 cards, with different texts. 4½ by 3½ ins. NET -------------- 12

Guiding Words. Floral cards, designed by a new artist. 12 cards, 12 texts. 4½ by 3¼ ins. NET------------------------- 12

Helps by the Way. Designs by BARONESS DE VOUGA. Elegantly printed. Each card has two texts, carefully selected. 12 cards, 4 by 6 ins. 24 texts. NET ----------------------- 15

33. Highway and Hedge Cards. 36 in a pack. 2¾ by 1¼ ins.-

66. Jewels. Floral cards with heads similar to No. 65. 12 cards, 3 by 4½ ins. 12 texts. NET--

2. Little Gems from the Mine. (BOOK MARKS.) 12 original water color designs, on finest cardboard, with charming texts. 3½ by 1¼ ins.---

65. Manna for the Day. 12 floral cords with heads of children, from designs by MISS LATHBURY. 12 cards, 3 by 4½ ins. 12 texts. NET---

5. Mottoes for the Memory from Holy Writ. A bright, sparkling, and beautiful packet of 12 cards. 3¾ by 2½ ins.-----

41. "Overcomes" of the Bible. Charming floral designs, with texts as indicated by the title. 12 cards, 12 texts. 5½ by 3 ins.-

4. Photograph Reward Cards. 2 packs of 12 cards each. A nice picture, a text, and verses on each card. 4 by 2½ ins. Per pack---

28. Picture Cards for Children. Neatly enveloped. In two packets, each 54 large cards. 5½ by 3½ ins. Per pack---------

27. Pocket Cards. 72 in a packet. 4 by 2¼ ins.--------------------

20. Precious Truths. 12 of the finest floral cards ever issued. Suited for older scholars. 4¾ by 3¾ ins.---------------------

34. Questions and Answers. A packet of 80 cards, questions with Bible answers. 3 by 2 ins.----------------------------------

Red and Blue Tickets. 125 on a sheet. Per sheet-----------

49. Sure Promises from God's Word. 72 cards, printed in colors, with texts--•

75. Texts and Symbols. A series of beautifully designed cards in 10 colors and gold, with texts and fitting symbols. Fitted with easel backs to stand upon table. 12 cards, 4¼ by 5½ ins.--------

70. Texts for the Infant Class. 200 cards. 1½ by ¾ ins. NET-

61. Thanksgivings. 1st Series. Elegant floral cards with texts. 24 cards, 24 texts. 3⅜ by 2½ ins. ----------------------------

62. Thanksgivings. 2d Series. Same general style as 1st series, but different designs and texts. 24 cards, 24 texts -------------

29. Thirty-six Picture Cards of the Life of Christ. With a colored border and a nice engraving, followed by Scripture on one side and a beautiful hymn on the other. 5½ by 3½ ins.-----

Vest Pocket Cards for Old and Young. 48 in a packet.
3½ by 2¼ ins. --- 10

Views in the Holy Land. A packet of 12 cards with easel
backs to stand upon table, with views of prominent scenes in
Bible Lands, wild flowers from the same country, and appropriate texts. 4¼ by 5½ ins. ---------------------------------- 25

Watchwords. 1st Series. Floral designs, with appropriate texts.
24 cards, 24 texts. 3⅜ by 2½ ins. ----------------------------- 15

Watchwords. 2d Series. Same kind of card as No. 59, but all
different. 24 cards, 24 texts. 3⅜ by 2½ ins. ------------------ 15

"Whosoevers" of the Bible. 12 cards of elegant roses,
with texts. 4½ by 3¼ ins. NET -------------------------------- 12

Words in Season. A packet of birds, flowers, and texts that
cannot fail to please and instruct. 12 cards. 3 by 4½ ins. ------ 15

Words of Eternal Life. Most elegant floral cards, original designs. 12 cards, 12 texts. 5 by 3¼ ins. NET ------------------ 12

Words of Faith. 12 fine floral cards, with different texts------ 20

Words of Grace. 1st Series. Charming floral designs. 12
cards, 12 texts. 5 by 3⅜ ins. -------------------------------- 20

Words of Grace. 2d Series. Different designs from 1st series.
12 cards, 12 texts. 5 by 3⅜ ins. ----------------------------- 20

Words of Promise. 1st Series. Floral cards, something en-
tirely new in designs. 12 cards, 12 texts. 5 by 3⅜ ins. -------- 20

Words of Promise. 2d Series. Same kind as 1st series, but
different designs and texts. 12 cards, 12 texts. 5 by 3⅜ ins. --- 20

Words of Strength. 12 cards, from original designs by BAR-
CLAY, with selections from Scripture. 5 by 3¼ ins. NET ------- 12

Words of the King. A packet from original designs with fine
flowers in twelve colors, special attention paid to the selection of
texts. 12 cards, 12 texts. 4 by 6 ins. NET-------------------- 15

Words of the Master. Some of the most beautiful flowers of
our own land, painted from nature by MISS BIRD. 12 texts, 12
cards in a packet. 3 by 5 ins. -------------------------------- 20

Words of Truth. Vases with flowers from original designs,
with texts. 12 texts, 12 cards. 5 by 4 ins. NET -------------- 12

Words for the Weary Ones. Four choice cards, beautifully
printed in colors, with readings from HAVERGAL and others.
4¾ by 7½ ins. --- 25

www.ingramcontent.com/pod-product-compliance
Lightning Source LLC
Chambersburg PA
CBHW021138020726
47500CB00003B/1140